Unité dans la Diversité

Unity in Diversity: French

Melanie Lotfali

~ Credits ~

Author & Illustrator   Melanie Lotfali

Translator   Jean-Paul Wattiaux

Version 1.3

ISBN 978-0-9873333-0-8

www.michelangela.com.au

Livres dans cette collection

Le Taïs de Dieu

God's Tais

Atesa, Akala, Aleki, Zenha and Abel love their parents. One day they decide to make a present for their parents. They go to buy some cotton to make tais.

Atesa, Akala, Aleki, Zenha et Abel aiment leurs parents. Un jour, ils décident de faire un cadeau à leurs parents. Ils vont acheter du coton pour faire des taïs.

Atesa's favorite
color is green.
She makes a green
tais. Akala likes
yellow. She makes a
yellow tais.

La couleur préférée
d'Atesa est le vert.
Elle fait un taïs vert.
Akala aime le jaune.
Elle fait un taïs
jaune.

LET'S ENJOY WITH THE COLOR INCREMENT OF COLOR.
FLOW

Aleki's favorite color is red. He uses red cotton to make a tais for his parents. Zenha thinks that pink is the most beautiful.

La couleur préférée d'Aleki est le rouge. Elle utilise du coton rouge pour faire un taïs pour ses parents. Zenha pense que le rose est bien plus beau.

Abel says that blue is
the best. He makes a
blue tais.

Abel dit que le bleu
est bien mieux. Il fait
un taïs bleu.

When they finish their taïs the children go and play. They leave the scraps of cotton on the ground.

Ameta walks past and finds the cotton left by the other children. She uses the cotton to make a taïs.

Lorsqu'ils ont fini leurs taïs, les enfants vont jouer. Ils laissent les restes de coton par terre.

Ameta passe par là et trouve le coton que les autres enfants ont laissé. Elle utilise ce coton pour faire un taïs.

Atesa's parents like
the green taïs that
Atesa made
for them.

Les parents d'Atesa
aiment le taïs vert
qu'Atesa leur a fait.

Akala, Aleki, Zenha
and Abel's parents
also like the yellow,
red, pink and blue
tais that their
children made
for them.

Les parents d'Akala,
Aleki, Zenha et
d'Abel aiment aussi
les taïs jaune, rouge,
rose et bleu que leurs
enfants leur ont faits.

English

But Ameta's parents were the happiest of all because their tais was made of many different colors.

Français

Mais les parents d'Ameta étaient les plus heureux car leur taïs était fait de différentes couleurs.

The people of the
world are many
different colors.
Different colored
cotton makes a taïs
more beautiful. And
different colored
people make our
world family more
beautiful.

Les gens dans le
monde sont de
différentes couleurs.
Des cotons de
couleurs différentes
font un taïs bien plus
beau. Et des gens de
couleurs différentes
rendent la famille du
monde bien plus belle.

The Earth is
but one country,
and mankind
its citizens.

~ Bahá'í Writings ~

La terre n'est
qu'un seul pays
et les hommes
en sont les citoyens.

~ Ecrits Bahá'í ~

L'Oeil qui Voulait Vivre Seul

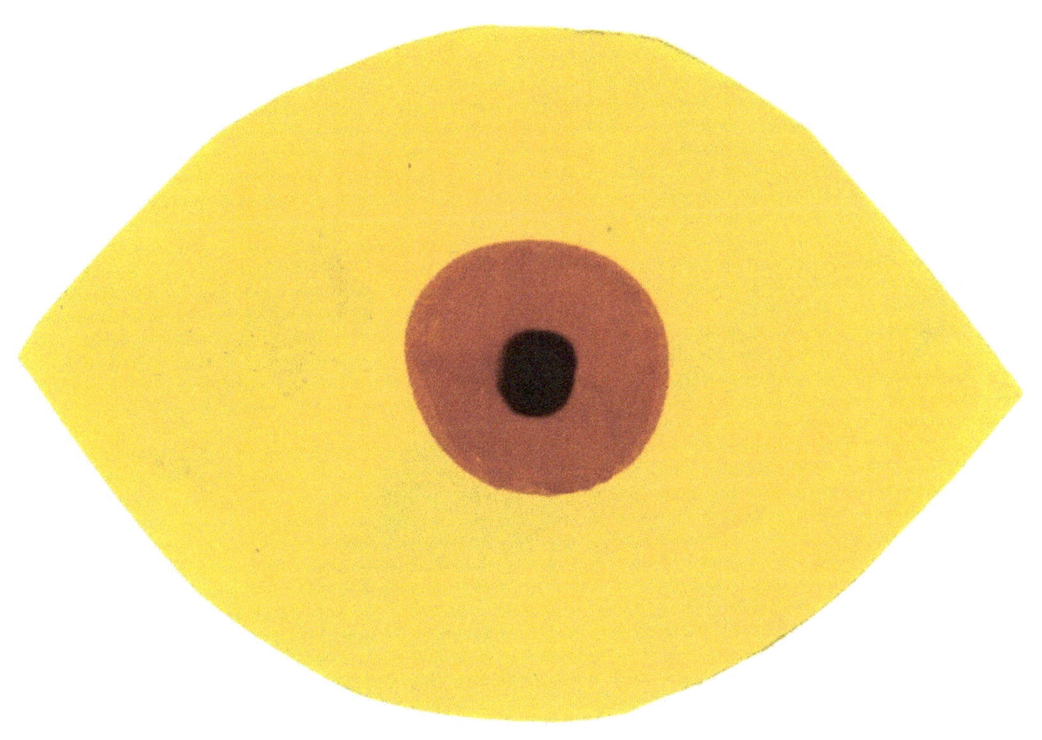

The Eye that Wanted to Live Alone

English

Once upon a time there lived a Body. This Body had all the things that bodies usually have, like two eyes, two hands, tummy, back, hair, ten fingers, and a bottom.

Français

Il était une fois un Corps. Ce Corps avait tout ce qu'un corps doit normalement avoir, deux yeux, deux mains, un ventre, un dos, des cheveux, dix doigts et un derrière.

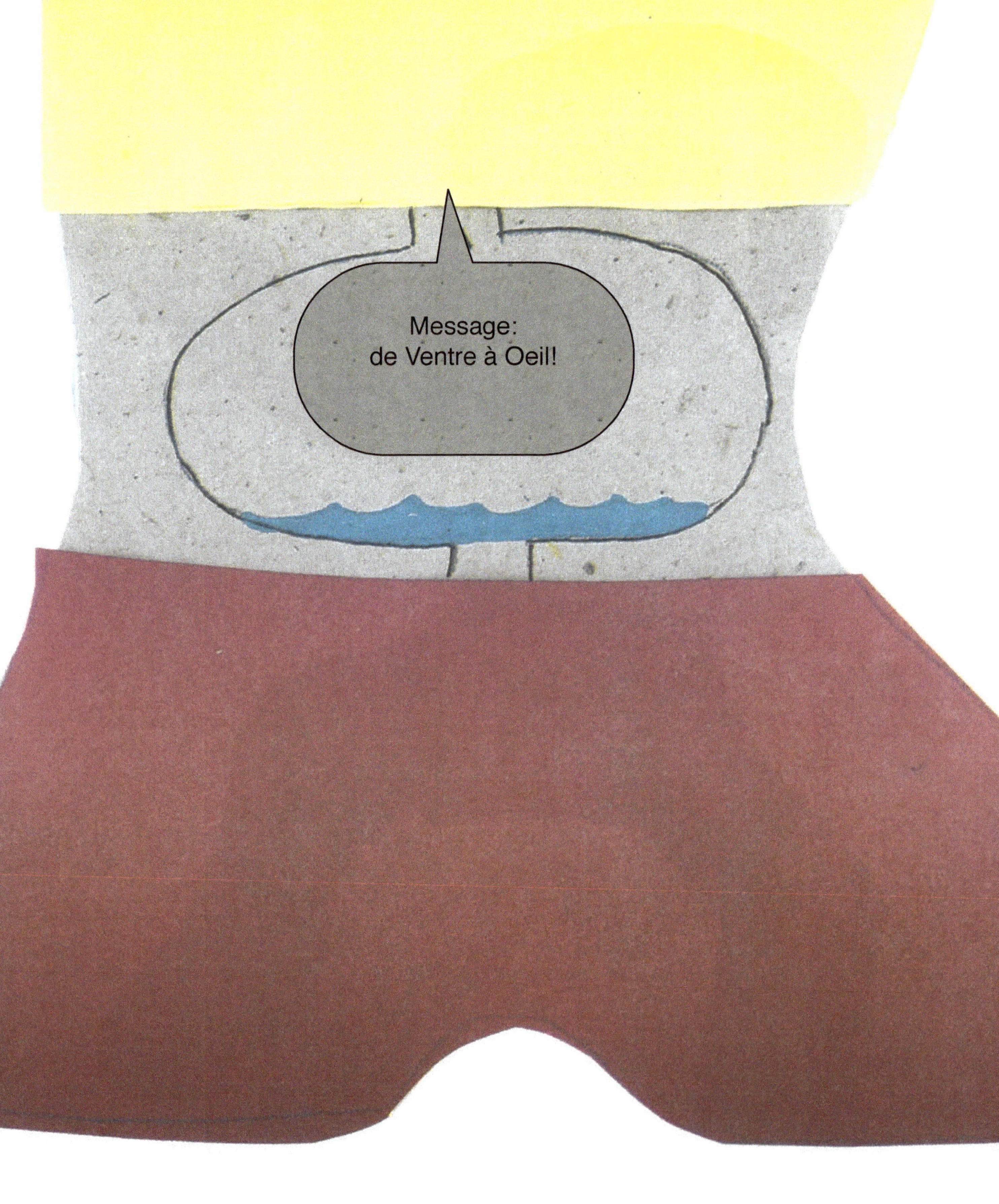
Message:
de Ventre à Oeil!

The parts of the Body were different and played different roles but they all worked together successfully.

For example, when Tummy felt empty, she told Eye to look for something to eat.

Les parties du Corps sont différentes et jouent des rôles différents mais elles travaillent ensemble avec succès.

Par exemple, lorsque le Ventre se sent vide, il dit à l'Oeil de chercher quelque chose à manger.

Eye looked for food and
then told Hand to take it.
Hand took the food,
Mouth opened and received
the food. Teeth chewed the
food and Tummy received
the food. Tummy turned it
into energy which it sent to
Arms and Legs so that
they could do their work.
And so, all the parts of the
body worked together
in harmony.

L'Oeil trouve de la
nourriture et dit à la Main
d'en prendre. La Main
prend la nourriture, la
Bouche s'ouvre et accepte
la nourriture. Les Dents
mâchent la nourriture et le
Ventre la reçoit. Le Ventre
transforme la nourriture en
énergie qui est envoyée
vers les Bras et les Jambes
pour leur permettre de faire
leur travail. Ainsi, toutes les
parties du corps travaillent
ensemble en harmonie.

But, one day, Eye started to think that she was more important than the other body parts.

She thought: "If I don't look for food, Hand doesn't know where to get it. Then, Mouth doesn't know to open and Tummy stays empty. I am the most important!"

Mais, un jour, l'Oeil commence à penser qu'il est plus important que les autres parties du corps.

Il pense: "Si je ne cherche pas de nourriture, la Main ne saura pas où en prendre. Alors la Bouche ne sait plus s'ouvrir et le Ventre reste vide. Je suis le plus important!"

Eye ordered the other body parts to call her Queen Eye.

She told them that she was the most important and they should honor her. But the other body parts didn't agree.

They said to Eye: "No, we all need each other. We all help each other and depend on each other."

L'Oeil donne l'ordre aux autres parties du corps de l'appeler Oeil-Roi.

Il leur dit qu'il est le plus important et qu'ils lui doivent le respect. Mais les autres parties du corps ne sont pas d'accord.

Elles disent à l'Oeil: "Non, nous avons tous besoin les uns des autres. Nous nous aidons tous les uns les autres et nous dépendons les uns des autres."

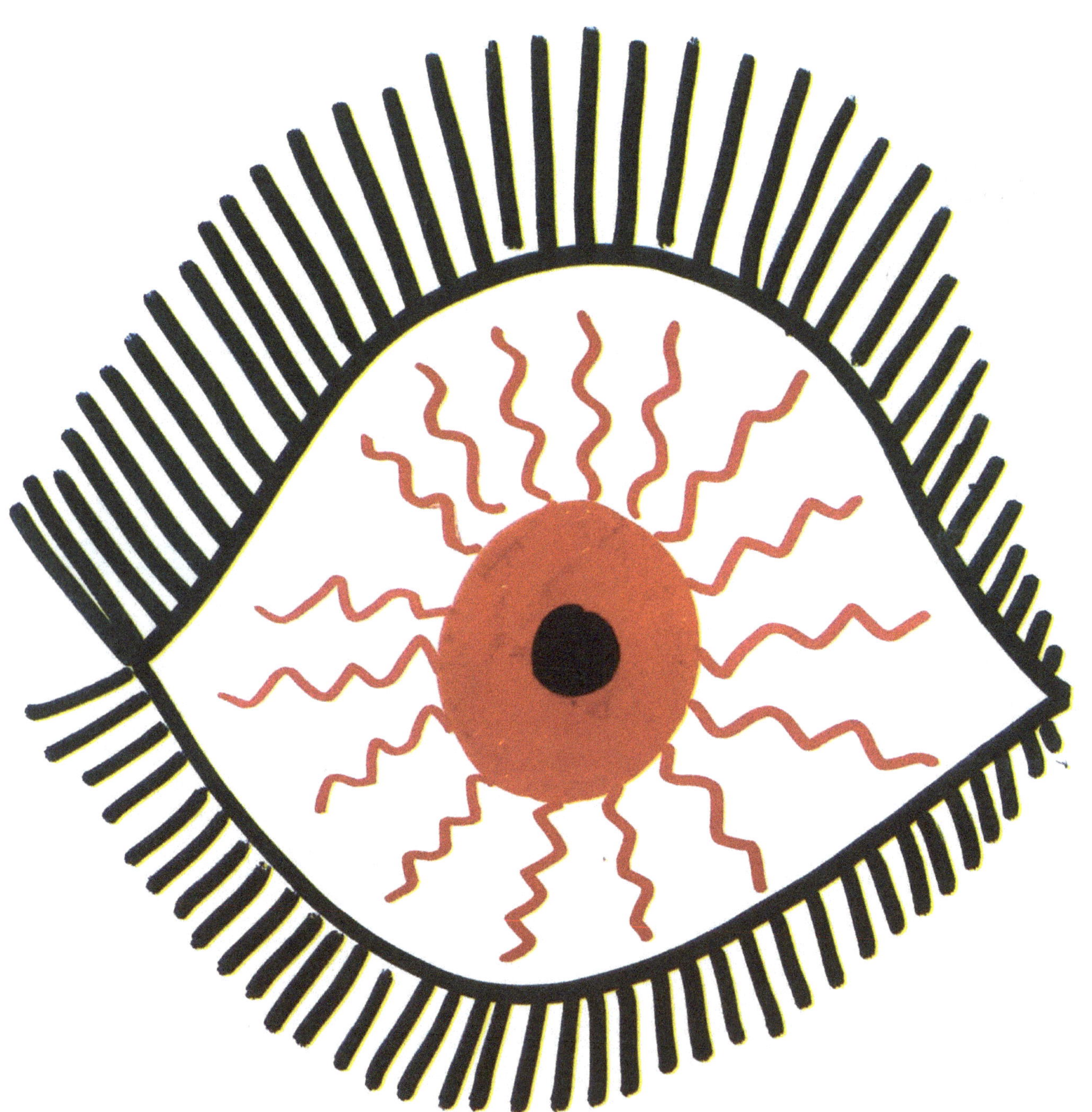

When Eye heard that they
didn't accept that she was
most important,
she was angry!

She said: **"If you don't
accept that I am queen,
and if you don't honor
me, I will not live
with you!"**

Quand l'Oeil entend qu'ils
n'acceptent pas qu'il soit
plus important, il se fâche!

Il dit: **"Si vous ne
m'acceptez pas comme
roi et si vous ne me
respectez pas, je ne
reste pas avec vous!"**

<table>
<tr><td>

Eye popped out of Face.
She went to live alone on
the table top.

</td><td>

L'Oeil quitte le visage. Il
veut vivre seul sur la table.

</td></tr>
</table>

The body parts felt very sad that Eye didn't want to live with them. A couple of hours later, Tummy felt empty. She sent a message to Eye's place, but there was no Eye.

So the message was sent directly to Hand. Hand received the message but didn't know what to do. He didn't know where to find food.

Les parties du corps sont fort tristes parce que l'Oeil ne veut pas vivre avec elles. Quelques heures plus tard, le Ventre se sent vide. Il envoie un message à l'endroit de l'Oeil. Mais l'Oeil n'y est plus.

Alors le message est envoyé directement à la Main. La Main reçoit le message mais ne sait pas quoi en faire. Elle ne sait pas où trouver de la nourriture.

Hand began to look for food by feeling. This took a long time but in the end he found a banana and gave it to Mouth. Mouth received it. Teeth chewed it. Tummy turned it into energy and sent it to Arms and Legs. Body suffered, but it didn't die.

La Main commence à chercher de la nourriture en touchant. Cela dure longtemps mais finalement elle trouve une banane et la donne à la Bouche. La Bouche l'accepte. Les Dents la mâchent. Le Ventre en fait de l'énergie qu'il envoie vers les Bras et les Jambes. Le Corps souffre mais ne meurt pas.

Meanwhile Eye sat alone on the table top. She sat and thought about how she was more important than the other parts. But after some time she also began to lose energy. Alone she could not get food, chew it or turn it into energy.

Pendant ce temps l'Oeil est seul sur la table. Il y est assis et il mesure à quel point il est plus important que les autres parties. Mais après quelque temps il commence aussi à manquer d'énergie. Seul il ne peut trouver de la nourriture, ni la mâcher, ni en faire de l'énergie.

English

In the end she was about to die. She called the Body and said: "Help me please. I am about to die."

The Body said to Eye: "You are right. You can't live alone. We need your help and you also need us. Let's help each other." Hand picked up Eye and put her back in Face.

Français

A la fin il est presque mourant. Il appele le Corps et dit: "Aide moi s'il te plait. Je vais mourir."

Le Corps dit à l'Oeil: "Tu as raison. Tu ne peux vivre seul. Nous avons besoin de ton aide et tu as aussi besoin de nous. Aidons-nous les uns les autres." La Main prend l'Oeil et le remet en place sur le visage.

Eye began to receive energy from the food that Tummy received from Hand and Mouth. Eye didn't die. She felt happy.

Eye said sorry to the other parts and said: "I made a mistake. You were right. We should all work together. We are all important, and we need unity to live well together."

L'Oeil commence à recevoir l'énergie de la nourriture que le Ventre reçoit grâce à la Main et à la Bouche. L'Oeil ne meurt pas. Il est heureux.

L'Oeil s'excuse auprès des autres parties et dit: "Je me suis trompé. Vous avez raison. Nous devons tous travailler ensemble. Nous sommes tous importants et nous avons besoin d'être unis pour bien vivre ensemble."

Be ye as the fingers
of one hand,
the members
of one body.

~ Bahá'í Writings ~

Soyez comme les doigts
d'une seule main,
les membres d'un
seul corps.

~ Ecrits Bahá'í ~

Koru Perfeitu Ida

A Perfect Chord

Indi-bird loved to sing. She knew how to sing one note. She sang it beautifully and with all her heart.

Indi-oiseau aimait chanter. Elle savait comment chanter une note. Elle chantait à merveille et de tout son coeur.

One day Jarrah-bird came to visit. He also knew how to sing one note. They sang together.

Un jour, Jarrah-oiseau lui rend visite. Il savait aussi comment chanter une note. Ils ont chanté ensemble.

Attracted by the sound, Tai-bird landed on the branch. He also knew how to sing just one note. It was different from the others. He added his note to the chord.

Attiré par le son, Tai-oiseau se pose sur la branche. Lui aussi savait comment chanter une seule note. Une note qui était différente de celles des autres. Sa note s'est ajoutée à l'accord.

Marama-bird heard the beautiful harmony of the three different notes.

"I can sing a note too," she chirped. She joined the group.

Marama-oiseau a entendu la merveilleuse harmonie des trois notes différentes.

"Je peux aussi chanter une note" dit-elle en pépiant. Elle s'est ajoutée au groupe.

Tama-bird flew in with a long loud "Cheeeeep Cheeeep". Joyfully he added his note to the music.

Tama-oiseau les rejoint avec un long et fort "Tchiiiip Tchiiiip". Avec joie il ajoute sa note à la musique.

The harmony of the different notes was like a magnet for Mihi and Skye. They glided over to the branch.

They opened their beaks and sang their notes. Each bird's note was different from the others. Each note was beautiful. Together they made the perfect chord.

L'harmonie des différentes notes était comme un aimant pour Mihi et Skye. Ils volent jusqu'à la branche.

Ils ouvrent leurs becs et chantent leurs notes. La note de chaque oiseau est différente des autres. Chaque note est merveilleuse. Ensemble ils font un accord parfait.

The diversity in the human
family should be the cause
of love and harmony, as it is
in music where many
different notes blend
together in the making of
a perfect chord.

~ Bahá'í Writings ~

La diversité dans la famille humaine devrait être cause d'amour et d'harmonie, comme en musique où beaucoup de notes différentes se mêlent en un accord parfait.

~ Ecrits Bahá'í ~

Les Étoiles d'un Seul Ciel

Stars of One Heaven

Clara was all alone. Clara was lonely. She looked up at the sky. She saw the sky was full of stars.

She turned to one and said: "You are so lucky. You have so many friends. I am all alone. I want a friend."

Clara était toute seule. Clara était isolée. Elle a regardé vers le ciel. Elle a vu que le ciel était plein d'étoiles.

Elle a dit à l'une d'elle: "Tu as beaucoup de chance. Tu as beaucoup d'amis. Je suis seule. Je voudrais une amie."

English	*Français*

Star said: "Clara, why don't you ask God for a friend?"

So Clara prayed. She asked God to send her a friend.

When she opened her eyes she saw that God had sent her a friend.

"Oh no!" said Clara. "I want a friend just like me! He is different from me!"

L'Étoile dit: "Clara, pourquoi ne demandes-tu pas à Dieu pour avoir une amie?"

Alors Clara a prié. Elle a demandé à Dieu de lui envoyer une amie.

Quand elle a ouvert es yeux elle, a vu que Dieu lui avait envoyé un ami.

"Oh non!" dit Clara. "Je veux un ami juste comme moi! Il est différent de moi!"

<table>
<tr><td>

English

Clara closed her eyes and prayed again. Then, she opened her eyes.

"Oh no!" sobbed Clara.

"I want a friend just like me! She is different from me!"

</td><td>

Français

Clara ferme es yeux et prie à nouveau. Puis, elle ouvre les yeux.

"Oh non!" sanglote Clara.

"Je veux une amie juste comme moi! Elle est différente de moi!"

</td></tr>
</table>

Clara closed her eyes and prayed again. Then, she opened her eyes.

"Oh no!" cried Clara. "I want a friend just LIKE ME! She is DIFFERENT from me!"

Clara threw herself on the grass. She cried and cried. The new friends wandered away.

Clara ferme les yeux et prie à nouveau. Puis elle ouvre les yeux.

"Oh non!" dit Clara en pleurant. "Je veux une amie juste COMME MOI! Elle est DIFFERENTE de moi!"

Clara se jette sur l'herbe. Elle pleure et pleure encore. Les nouveaux amis, eux se sont éloignés.

That night she turned to Star. "Why does God keep sending me the wrong thing?" she asked.

Star said to Clara: "When you look up to the sky, what do you see?"

Cette nuit là, elle dit à l'Etoile: "Pourquoi Dieu ne m'envoie jamais que ce qui ne me convient pas?"

L'Etoile dit à Clara: "quand tu regardes le ciel que vois-tu?"

Clara said: "I see beautiful stars shining brightly."

Star said: "That's right. We are all different shapes, colors, and sizes. But when you look up you see our unity. You see we are all stars."

Clara dit: "Je vois de belles étoiles brillantes et étincelantes."

L'Etoile dit: "C'est bien cela. Nous sommes toutes différentes par la forme, la couleur et la taille. Mais quand tu regardes, tu vois notre unité. Tu vois nous sommes toutes des étoiles."

English

"When I look down," said Star, "I see beautiful human beings. It doesn't matter that you are different shapes, colors, and sizes. You are all human beings."

"Oh yes!" laughed Clara.

"Now, where did they go, those friends just like me?"

Français

"Quand je regarde en bas" dit l'Etoile, "je vois des êtres humains merveilleux. Peu importe vos différences de forme, de couleur ou de taille. Vous êtes tous des êtres humains."

"Oh oui!" dit Clara en riant. "Maintenant, où sont-elles ces amies qui sont juste comme moi?"

...love will make
them all the stars
of one heaven.

~ Bahá'í Writings ~

...cet amour fera

d'eux les étoiles

d'un seul ciel.

~ Ecrits Bahá'í ~

Les Fruits d'un Même Arbre

The Fruit of One Tree

When I get up I see our fruit bowl. It is full of ripe yellow bananas. Today I want to eat bananas for breakfast, lunch, and dinner. I peel a banana and take a big bite.

Quand je me lève, je vois notre coupe de fruits. Elle est pleine de bananes jaunes et mûres. Aujourd'hui je veux manger des bananes au petit déjeuner, au déjeuner et au dîner. Je péle une banane et en mange un gros morceau.

English

Then I see Maria selling mangos. I remember how sweet and slimy they are. Maria sells me some mangos.

Français

Puis je vois Maria qui vend des mangues. Je me souviens de leur goût sucré et juteux. Maria me vend quelques mangues.

When I go to the tap to wash the mango juice from my chin, I see our paw paw tree. Paw paw with lime juice. My favourite!

Lorsque je vais au robinet pour laver le jus de mangue de mon menton, je vois notre papayer. Une papaye avec du jus de citron. C'est ce que je préfère!

Even with my belly full of paw paw, the orange tree catches my eye. I pull an orange off the branch. I peel it and break the orange ball into pieces. I put them in my mouth one by one.

Même avec le ventre plein de papaye, je remarque l'oranger. Je cueille une orange. Je la pèle et je sépare les quartiers que je mets en bouche un par un.

I start to think:
Bananas are yummy.
Mangos are sweet.
Paw paws are
delicious. Oranges
are tasty.

Je commence à
réfléchir. Les bananes
sont succulentes. Les
mangues sont sucrées.
Les papayes sont
délicieuses. Les
oranges sont
savoureuses.

What if we put them together? What if we ate them mixed together? That would be the best of all.

Et si on les mettait ensembles? Ou si on les mangeait mélangées? Ce serait mieux que tout.

Yummy, sweet, delicious, tasty Fruit Salad!

Miam-miam, une délicieuse salade de fruits sucrés et savoureux!

O people of the world,
ye are all the fruit of
one tree and the leaves
of one branch.

~ Bahá'í Writings ~

O peuple du monde,
vous êtes les fruits
d'un même arbre
et les feuilles d'une
même branche.

~ Ecrits Bahá'í ~

Fellowship Farm

Volume 1: BOOKS 1-3

Leezah, Skye-Maree and Olingah Fitzgerald live with their parents on Fellowship Farm. In the first book of the Fellowship Farm series, you will meet the children and learn about their daily activities on the farm. There is a lot to be done each day: pillow fights, morning prayers, pig feeding and school bus riding. They help their dad feed the cows, add stickers to their virtues poster and learn to deal with bullies.

Then you will join the Fitzgerald children on their many adventures with puppies, snake bites, treasure hunts, bonfires, camping by the sea, and tree houses. And as they go they sometimes practice their virtues, and sometimes forget…

Suitable for independent readers aged 8-12 years; parent-read from six years. Order online from print-on-demand services, and digitally from the iBookstore or Kindle.

Fellowship Farm

Volume 2: BOOKS 4-6

Leezah, Skye-Maree and Olingah Fitzgerald live with their parents on Fellowship Farm. In the first volume of the Fellowship Farm series, you met the children and learned about their daily activities on the farm.

In this the second volume the Fitzgerald children are visited by their cousins, Nick and Anisa. Together they travel by horse and cart to the market, attend the 19 Day Feast, go camping, find a pirate map and treasure, as well as experience the intensity of crisis and victory when Olingah's life is put in serious danger.

Suitable for independent readers aged 8-12 years; parent-read from six years. Order online from print-on-demand services, and digitally from the iBookstore or Kindle.

Fellowship Farm

Volume 3: BOOKS 7-9

In this, the third volume of stories about Leezah, Skye-Maree and Olingah Fitzgerald who live with their parents on Fellowship Farm, the children set out with joy to go blackberry picking.

But an unexpected turn of events at the river makes them fear for the lives of their puppies. Ayyám-i-Há follows with serving, teaching, gifts, treasure-hunts as well as the challenge of bullying for Skye-Maree. After Ayyám-i-Há comes an opportunity to visit their eccentric Uncle Jack who takes them to the chocolate factory, aquatic centre and gives them many other treats both spiritual and edible!

Suitable for independent readers aged 8-12 years; parent-read from six years. Order online from print-on-demand services, and digitally from the iBookstore or Kindle.

Fellowship Farm

Volume 4: BOOKS 10-12

In the fourth volume of stories about Leezah, Skye-Maree and Olingah Fitzgerald of Fellowship Farm they prepare for the annual Naw Ruz Mahta River Boat Race. There are some unexpected hitches.

Skye-Maree and Olingah learn about loyalty and sacrifice as they work out how to respond to the challenges they face. Soon after Naw Ruz winter sets in and the family rug up and head for the ski slopes.

Along the way they experience the life-threatening danger of losing unity, the challenge of learning to ski, the power of prayer, and patience in the face of frustration. They meet funny Magic, the back to front panda, and suffer some bruises. Their patience is well rewarded when their parents announce that a dear wish of the children is to be fulfilled.

Suitable for independent readers aged 8-12 years; parent-read from six years. Order online from print-on-demand services, and digitally from the iBookstore or Kindle.

Unity in Diversity

This brightly illustrated picture book contains five simple stories for young readers. They foster an understanding of the oneness of the human race and celebrate its diversity within that unity.

Likening the human race to various colored cotton in a woven cloth, various fruits on the tree of life, stars in the heavens, members of one body, and different notes in one perfect chord, the stories use the concrete to teach the abstract.

Young readers will enjoy the bright colors and simple text as they develop their understanding of the unity and diversity of the human race.

Ideal for children aged 4-8 years.
Order online from print-on-demand services, and digitally from the iBookstore. Translated into French, Portuguese, Romanian, Tetum, and Mongolian.

The Big Story

The Big Story explains the way in which the divinely ordained and guided process that has brought human beings into existence has taken place gradually over time and space. It shows that the concepts of evolution and creation are not mutually exclusive.

Science and religion are shown to be two windows on one reality, two knowledge systems that when properly understood, function as one cohesive whole.

This book is most suitable for readers 14 years and older. Younger readers will enjoy the bright and informative illustrations but will require support to understand the text.

Suitable for independent readers aged 14+ years; with assistance from 12+. Order online from print-on-demand services, and digitally from the iBookstore.

Dr Melanie Lotfali

Author of The Fitzgeralds of Fellowship Farm series and Unity in Diversity series.

Melanie Lotfali PhD is a graduate of the Australian College of Journalism in Professional Writing for Children. She is the author of eighteen books of fiction and non-fiction for children and the illustrator of five.

Melanie has taught spiritual education classes for children for the past twenty years in five countries and is currently an active animator and trainer of animators for the Junior Youth Spiritual Empowerment Program. She is a qualified counselor and classroom teacher, and for the past six years has facilitated violence prevention and respectful relationships programs in high schools.

Much of her childhood was spent on the farms, beaches and mountains of Tasmania, where the Fellowship Farm series is set. As an adult she spent four years in Siberia and four years in East Timor as a pioneer.

She currently lives in Lismore, Australia, with her family.

Michael Cohen

Author of The Big Story and publisher of all Michelangela books.

Michael Cohen graduated as a Computer Systems Engineer in 1990 and worked for many years in software design and informations systems. He changed careers in 2008 to become a Registered Nurse working in the area of Mental Health and Alcohol & Other Drugs.

Michael has been a keen participant in and advocate of the programs offered by **The Foundation for the Application and Teaching of the Sciences** (FUNDAEC) and **Institute for Studies in Global Prosperity** (ISGP). He strives to contribute to processes and discourses leading to the progress of humankind toward a world society characterized by unity, justice and equity. A fundamental premise of Michael's worldview is that true science and true religion are necessarily in harmony, indeed are two windows on one reality. His writing seeks to promote understanding of this liberating concept and to contribute to a civilization that is ever advancing materially and spiritually.

He currently lives in Lismore, Australia, with his family.

Michelangela

website - www.michelangela.com.au
email - info@michelangela.com.au

To receive Michelangela's occasional
product announcements
please visit our website and
enter your email address and name
via the subscribe button

Warm Regards,
Melanie & Michael of Michelangela.

www.ingramcontent.com/pod-product-compliance
Lightning Source LLC
Chambersburg PA
CBHW041209100726
47911CB00017B/901